ALONG CAME BUTCH

D.J. LAWRENCE

Archway Publishing books may be ordered through booksellers or by contacting:

Archway Publishing
1663 Liberty Drive
Bloomington, IN 47403
www.archwaypublishing.com
844-669-3957

ISBN: 978-1-6657-3496-7 (sc)
ISBN: 978-1-6657-3498-1 (hc)
ISBN: 978-1-6657-3497-4 (e)

Print information available on the last page.

Archway Publishing rev. date: 12/19/2022

Books by D.J. Lawrence

Baking with Nana
A Cold Winter's Day

Dedicated to my granddaughter Izzy
who inspired me to write this story.

Have you ever read a fairy tale where there is a magical genie that makes things happen for a little princess? Well, it is just that, a fairy tale where anything goofy can happen.

Oh sure, go ahead and laugh but my name is Butch, and I am a flea.

Do you remember the time you had a difficult issue in math class this past school year and you scratched your head trying to think of the answer to your dilemma?

Well, that was me making your head itch to help you think clearly. And it worked!

When I was born, I was the 21st egg in the cluster. Clusters normally do not exceed twenty eggs and as a result I suffer from FBS... Flea Biting Syndrome which means I don't have the ability to bite like the other fleas.

So, I'm a non-biting pest, but I can sure make a mess out of an apple.

As a minor league pest, I graduated from FMAIL - Flea Mobile Advanced Institute of Learning.

Yes, we became the next generation after email.

So, I was given the assignment to help people like you move from one grade to the next.

Specifically, to help young people moving from the second grade to the third grade.

2 Fleas x 3 = 6 Fleas

Those were two of my best grades in Flea School so Mrs Flea Bag, the principal thought they could best use me to aid others during that school period.

It feels like I just got out of Flea School, but is has been a long time since that period in my fly by night lifetime but those were good times for me.

I didn't get in Miss Crabtree's class with my friend Spanky and the rest of the gang, I got in Miss Flyswatter's class.

Miss Flyswatter kept us on track by keeping the air stirred around us pushing us to think clearly and be alert.

If not, she would propel us across
the room with one swift swat.

.So, what's on your mind? Yep, I want to know what you want to know. Sound like double talk? It's not. I am sure numerous times throughout the day stuff jumps into your brain waves such as "what makes a cloud show up in the sky?"

You know stuff like that.

You have it much easier than most people because you live in the computerized era. Not everyone may have a laptop, but most have cellphones letting them reach into the internet for answers to questions, so your phone is a portable computer.

Why can't dogs eat chocolate?

Where do birds go during a storm?

How many people live in the U.S.A.?

If all the ice in a glass of ice water were
to melt, will the glass overflow?

Computers make reading and learning easier. If I had a computer when I was in flea class, I may have been able to grow up to be a dragon fly, rather than the pest that I am as a flea.

But that's who I am and proud of it.

Okay, let's get back into the clouds.

So, you are in the backyard weeding around some flowers.

Yes, you are helping Mom in her new flower garden, and you looked up and saw some fluffy white clouds developing. Do you know why or how they develop?

Okay, quit daydreaming and stay focused
on the why and how of clouds. Rest assured;
good old Butch didn't make them.

Clouds are a visible mass of liquid droplets, frozen crystals or particles suspended in the atmosphere. Now that definition, which you can find if you google the word "clouds", says a mass of minute liquid droplets. You know "minute" which is a sixtieth of an hour but in this case, it is actually pronounced "mi nute". You know something even smaller than a flea like me.

Years ago, you would have to go to the library and use encyclopedias which are made up of several volumes of large books usually one book for each letter of the alphabet, so if you want to look up the word "cloud" you would get volume "C".

Unfortunately, you could not look up questions such as "how do cloud come and go?" But with computers you can pose more specific questions making the learning process easier and fun.

So yes, let your fingers do the walking.

Reading is a great escape from your normal routine. It lets you role play, you know, become someone else just like when you and your friend played teacher and principle. Some people become writers which provides them the ability to create any role they desire. Reading and writing are major parts of life as they add experience and knowledge to each of us.

Reading and writing require an attitude that is very important to our development as a person, even to a flea like me. After all I could have been assigned to a dog and then a flea collar would have been the end of me.

So now you have completed the second grade and are preparing for the third. What you begin to learn in third grade will build upon what you learned in the second grade. It's like a set of building blocks.

<u>Algebra</u> <u>World History</u> <u>Civics</u> <u>Sports</u>
<u>Cooking</u> <u>Political Science</u> <u>Writing</u> <u>Religion</u>
<u>Adding</u> <u>Subtracting</u> <u>Gym</u> <u>Math</u> <u>Science</u> History

The higher you can build upward is based on the strength of your foundation. The funny part is the more you challenge yourself to learn new things by reading and writing, the easier it becomes.

Throughout the day as you see something or hear something that catches your attention, make a note, and google it.

Those small searches can lead into larger searches. Keep some notes or maybe put

together a binder on what you found during your research.

Okay, time to go to work and prepare for the third grade.

I need to go and make someone itch but will be back to check on your progress. I see a horse going by so maybe I'll jump onto him and go for a ride. Until then I won't bug you.

Butch